Copyright © 2002 by Melanie Eclare
All rights reserved

Published in the United States by Ragged Bears
413 Sixth Avenue
Brooklyn, New York 11215
www.raggedbears.com

Simultaneously published in the United Kingdom by Ragged Bears
Milborne Wick, Sherborne, Dorset DT9 4PW

CIP Data is available

First Edition
Printed and bound in China
ISBN: 1-929927-31-2
10 9 8 7 6 5 4 3 2 1

Ragged Bears wishes to thank Matthew Davis, Children's Garden
Coordinator, Hawthorne Valley Farm Visiting Students Program,
for generously sharing his knowledge of gardening and his years
of experience in creating gardens with children.

A Harvest of Color

GROWING A VEGETABLE GARDEN

Melanie Eclare

RAGGED BEARS

BROOKLYN, NEW YORK · MILBORNE WICK, DORSET

Introduction

It is early spring, and some of my friends, my little brother, Freddie, and I decide to make a garden on an empty patch of land. We want to grow vegetables.

They not only look good and smell good, but they taste good too. At the end of the summer, we will have a big feast.

We bring our tools to the garden to get the soil ready for planting. First we dig it up and turn it over until it is nice and crumbly. Then we rake it free of rocks. Then we decide which vegetables to plant. Each of us is in charge of one vegetable, except for me, Sophie. Freddie is so little that he and I will grow one together. And all of us will help each other. We decide to keep garden diaries and take photos as we go along. Here is a record of how our neighborhood vegetable garden grew.

Molly's Carrots

I love carrots because they are sweet and crunchy. And I can share them with my pet rabbit.

I sprinkled seeds into rows as deep as my thumbnail. We planted three rows of carrots, each one as far apart as the distance from the end of my middle finger to my elbow. To be sure the rows were straight, we attached string to two sticks and put them in the soil at each end of the garden bed. After we put the seeds into the ground, we covered the rows with soil and watered them. In about ten days little plants that looked like ferns showed through the soil. There were so many of them that I had to pull some out, which is called thinning. The seedlings that are left after thinning have enough room to grow into strong plants that make large healthy carrots.

Carrots grow underground. We all wanted to see them growing, but carrots are like a birthday present that can't be opened early. We dug up some carrots three different times before we had some that were big enough to eat.

MOLLY'S TIPS ON MEASURING A GARDEN

Gardens look nice when vegetables are evenly spaced. Seed packages give helpful directions on how far apart to sow seeds.

An easy way to be sure your rows are even is to measure yourself and use your measurements as a guide. Then you won't have to bother with rulers. Here are some measurements I find helpful:

* Distance across one finger.
* Distance across two fingers.
* Distance from the tip of my index finger to my wrist.
* Distance from my wrist to my elbow.
* The length of my foot.
* The width of my hand with my thumb and fingers spread out.
* The length of my arm.
* The length of my thumbnail.

Everyone is a different size and has different measurements, so be sure to find out what yours are!

Sam's Radishes

Radishes are my favorite vegetable because they are spicy and hot, all at the same time. You can eat them whole or slice them for a salad. I like them whole best.

Radishes grow fast. We planted them in rows as deep as half my thumbnail. Then we covered them with soil and watered them, and in only three days we saw small green leaves showing above the ground. I gave them more water, but I didn't let the ground get muddy. One day after I watered them, I found a worm crawling through the plants. Everyone said that meant the soil was healthy, so I put it back where I found it.

Three weeks later, Sophie pulled a small perfect radish. I decided they would be better if they were bigger, so I left them in the ground for another week.

The radishes are ready after four weeks. Sophie and Freddie tried them at the same time. Not everyone likes radishes!

SAM'S TIPS ON GROWING RADISHES

* I planted radish seeds in soil as deep as half my thumbnail and as far apart as the width of one of my fingers.

* I made the rows the same distance as the span of my hand from my thumb to my little finger when they are stretched as wide as possible.

* I used sticks and string to be sure the rows were straight.

* When I saw the first leaves of the radish plants, I thinned them so they were as far apart as three of my fingers side by side, just the way Molly thinned her carrots.

Robert's Potatoes

Baked potatoes with sour cream! French fries! Potatoes are so good, I forget they are vegetables!

Potatoes don't grow from seeds. Instead, they grow from pieces of old potatoes. Over the winter, Sophie saved some potatoes in a cool, dry place—an unheated room in the basement of her house. We cut the old potatoes into pieces and made holes in the garden as deep as the space from the tip of my index finger to my wrist. Then we dropped in pieces of old potato and patted the soil over them firmly. Under the ground, the potato pieces sent out shoots that formed new potatoes.

On top of the ground, plants with green leaves appeared in three weeks. When potatoes are fully grown, they are dug out of the ground with a special fork.

Potatoes take a long time to grow. We planted them in early spring, and three months later, we started to dig them. Because they grow underground and you can't see them before you harvest them, you never know whether they will be large or small. We got some of each.

ROBERT'S TIPS ON GROWING POTATOES

* Potatoes need a lot of space. I made the rows as far apart as the length of my arm, and six hand spans separated the individual plants.

* When the potato leaves show above the ground, it's time to 'hill' them. To do this, use a hoe to push the soil up to the first leaves of the plant. The hills protect the potatoes that are growing close to the surface of the soil from sunlight. Sunlight turns potatoes green, and green potatoes are poisonous.

* You have to be patient to grow potatoes. Sam grew three crops of radishes in the same amount of time it took my potatoes to grow.

Sophie and Freddie's Zucchini

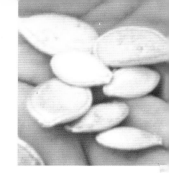

Freddie and I decided to work on our part of the vegetable garden together. We grew zucchini. Actually, neither of us likes zucchini, but our mother does. We want to make her some zucchini bread and maybe even some zucchini pancakes.

We started our plants indoors during the cold weather. We planted the zucchini seeds in a seed tray, which we put in a sunny window. Freddie and I took turns making sure the seeds had enough water. When the weather warmed up, we took the young plants outdoors to add to the garden. We dug holes that measured from the tip of my index finger to my wrist and placed the plants in them. We patted the soil firmly around the plants.

Because zucchini become very large plants, we gave the seedlings plenty of room to grow. Freddie took ten steps, heel to toe, to measure the space for each of the seedlings I planted. Then we watered them well. The plants grew fast. Within three weeks we started picking and cooking zucchini.

Zucchini grow fast. First you see leaves, then a beautiful golden blossom. A few days later, the blossom starts to curl up, and a fresh, tender green squash is in its place. Some people like to pick and cook the blossoms, some like the squash, and some like both.

SOPHIE AND FREDDIE'S TIPS ON GROWING ZUCCHINI

* Start your seeds indoors about a month before you expect the last frost.

* Plant the seedlings outside when you are sure there is no chance of frost and the ground feels warm.

* Pick the zucchini often. This keeps the plants healthy, and the more you pick, the more they grow.

Alex's Beans

Beans are the only vegetable that I like, so that's what I chose to grow.

I planted bean seedlings indoors during the cold weather, just the way Sophie and Freddie grew zucchini. When the weather turned warm, we took the bean seedlings outdoors to plant. With the help of grownups, supports for the beans to grow on were put in place. Then we dug holes next to the supports that were as deep as the distance from the tip of my index finger to my wrist. We placed the bean seedlings in the holes as far apart from each other as the distance between two spans of my hand with the thumb and fingers spread apart as far as they would go. We patted soil around them, watered them, and started the vines up the supports. After a week the leaves looked like they were being eaten. We all wondered what could be wrong. We learned that slugs were eating the plants. Luckily we found most of them before they ate too many of the vines, and the plants soon looked better. In ten weeks, the first small beans appeared. A week later, they were ready to be picked.

Everyone helped pick the beans. They were so good that we ate them raw right there in the garden.

ALEX'S TIPS ON GROWING BEANS

* There are many ways to support beans. One of the easiest and most fun is to set tall bean poles in a circle.

* Leave an opening on one side for a doorway. Tilt the poles inward and tie them together at the top where they meet. As the plants grow up the poles, they form a tepee with walls of bright green leaves.

* Like zucchini, once beans are ready to be harvested, pick them often, and the plants will continue to produce throughout the warm weather.

By the end of the summer, we had a wonderful garden! We celebrated with a cookout, and we made a vegetable salad that included everything that Molly, Sam, Robert, Alex, Freddie and I grew. Here is our recipe. Before you start, be sure you have a big pot and a grown up to help in cutting and cooking the vegetables.

You will need:
12 potatoes
4 carrots, sliced
12 radishes, sliced
2-3 small zucchini, sliced
1 lb. string beans,
broken into bite-sized pieces
1/2 cup tarragon vinegar
2 tbs. Dijon mustard
1 cup olive oil
salt and pepper

2 to 3   2 to 6
2 3 4 5 6

Wash all the vegetables and chop or slice them. Boil the potatoes until they are tender (15-20 minutes). Allow them to cool and cut into bite-sized pieces. Steam the beans for 5-8 minutes. Steam the zucchini for 2 minutes. Put all the vegetables in a large bowl. Mix together the vinegar, salt and pepper. Add the mustard. Add the olive oil and pour over the vegetables. Mix well. Serve and enjoy!